I CAN'T WAIT UNTIL I'M

OLD ENOUGH TO HUNT WITH DAD

written by Scott Johnson
illustrated by Karen Johnson

Printed in Mexico

ISBN 1-887251-56-1

Library of Congress Catalog Card Number: 95-92393

DEDICATION

This book is lovingly dedicated to my three daughters Keri, Robin,
and Leanne, and especially to my wife Karen, who coached me through
the slow publication process. May my daughters respect and hunt the
wildlife as I have.

Special thanks to Stephen D. Carpenteri, editor of New England Game
& Fish. Without his advice and challenges this book might not have
been written.

When autumn comes and the leaves are turning bright yellows and reds, Dad gets really excited because he knows deer season is coming. Dad shoots his bow and arrow every night after supper. He let's me shoot with him until Mom calls me in to get ready for bed. We see who can shoot the most bull's eyes. Dad says he would never shoot at a deer unless he was absolutely sure he could hit it. That's why he practices shooting every night.

On the weekends Dad takes me into the woods to find a hunting spot. He says we are looking for a spot in between where the deer hide and sleep and where they eat. Dad says it is a game of hide and seek. The deer hide and the hunter seeks.

Dad says the deer hide in the thickets. This is a place that is so thick with small trees and brush that it is hard to walk through. It is a dark and secret place.

The deer eat many things. Dad says apples, acorns, and grasses are their favorite snacks. They also love the shoots of woody plants.

After we've found where the deer hide and where they eat, Dad says we have to find a place nearby to sit. He says it has to be a place where the deer will walk past us either going to eat or going back to their hiding place. Dad says that it has to be a place where the deer won't see or smell us. He says that is the secret to winning the hide and seek game.

Whative a good place to sit is found and hunting season is open, it is time to hunt. Dad walks to his secret spot before the morning light. He says that way he can be sitting before the woods' creatures are awake. He says that just before the sun comes up, the woods' creatures all wake up at the same time. He says that it is as though a switch was turned on telling the creatures to awake.

By listening and watching the woods' creatures, Dad says they will tell you when a deer is approaching. The squirrels will scurry up the trees and the chipmunks will crawl into their holes. He says the squirrels will bark excitedly from the trees and the bluejays will scold them.

When the deer finally arrives, Dad carefully aims and shoots. He says the arrow will kill the deer quickly.

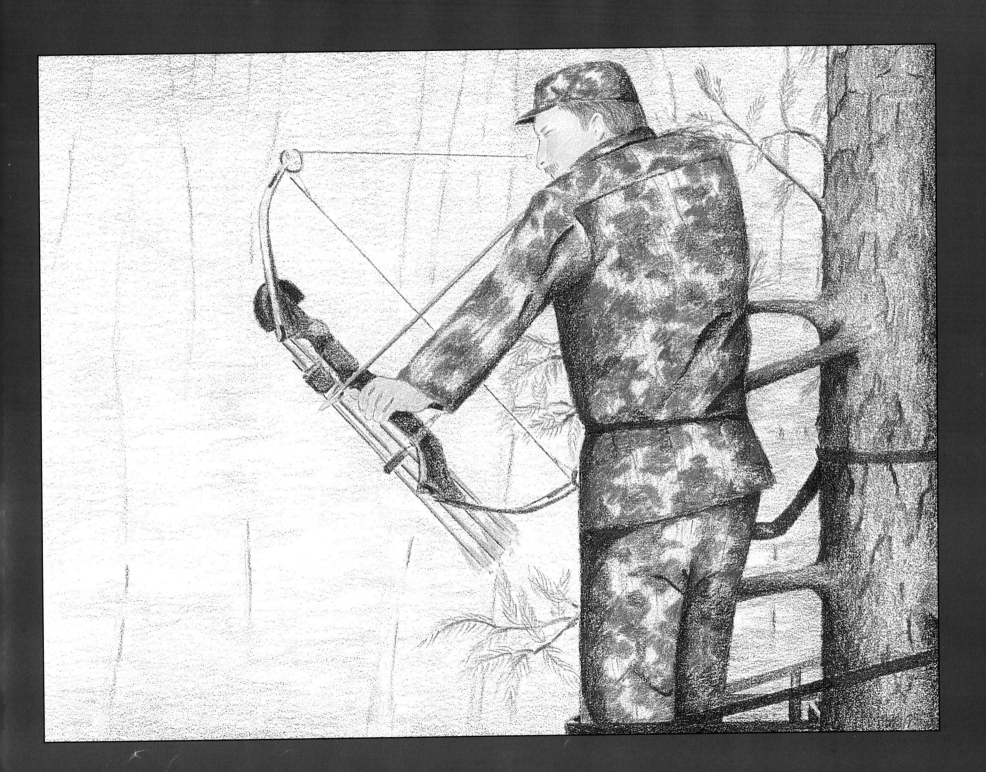

When Dad brings the deer home, he skins it and cuts it into steaks and chops. Mom cooks the meat for supper and makes jerky, a chewy snack the Indians used to make. Mom has the deerskin made into warm winter gloves. Nothing on the deer goes to waste.

After the hunting season is over, Dad cleans and oils his bow and puts his arrows away. We talk about all the bull's eyes we got while shooting and all the fun we had walking in the woods.

I can't wait until I'm old enough to hunt with Dad.

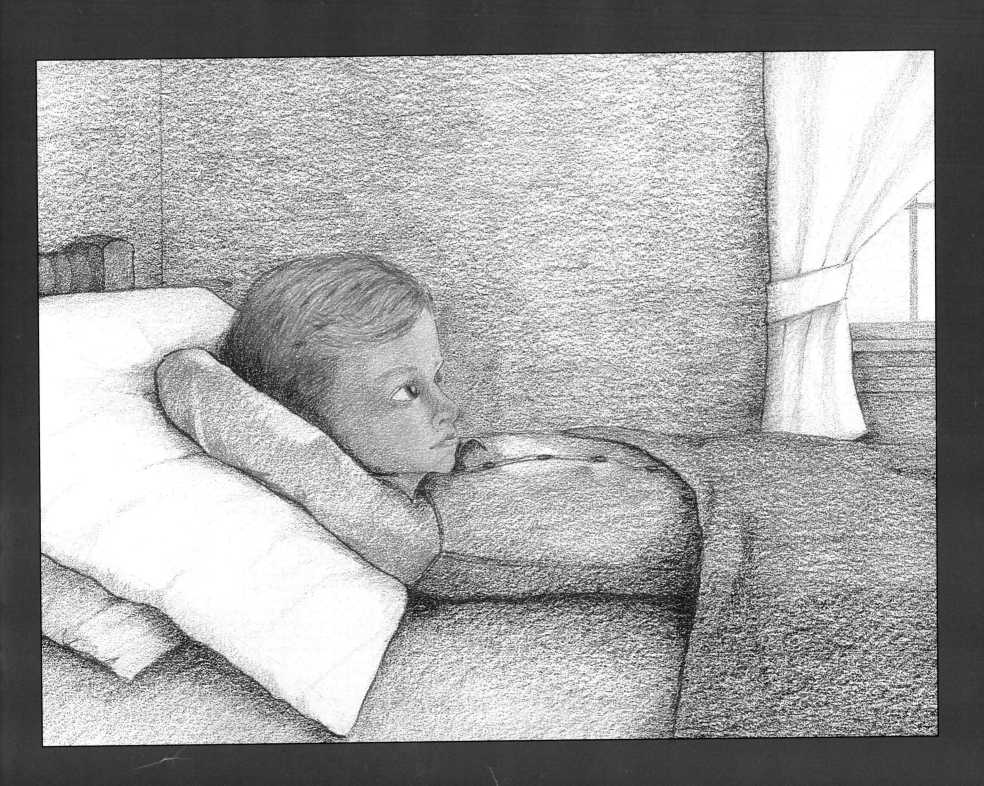